D1407269

HARD LINES 2

HARD LINES 2

ff

faber and faber

LONDON · BOSTON

First published in 1985
by Faber and Faber Limited
3 Queen Square London WC1N 3AU

Filmset by Wilmaset Birkenhead
Printed in Great Britain by
Whitstable Litho Ltd Whitstable Kent
All rights reserved

British Library Cataloguing in Publication Data

Hard lines.——2
1. English poetry——20th century
821'.914'08   PR1225
ISBN 0–571–13542–0

Library of Congress Cataloging in Publication Data

Hard lines 2.
1. English literature——20th century.   I. Dury, Ian.
PR1150.H36   1985   820'.8'00914   85–1549

ISBN 0–571–13542–0

INTRODUCTION

The criminal is the creative artist; the policeman is merely a critic.
                                                    G. K. CHESTERTON

Notes on item choosing and hopes that grow by leaps and bounds, with one or two suggestions:

F. Dubes, S. Hardie, P. Townshend, A. Bleasdale and I. Durex made this selection for *Hard Lines 2* from a short list of 200 pieces previously picked by Hardie and Dubes from over 83 million entries.

We each first read the works at home, then met at the publisher's to make the final dongler with warm argument and loud readings.

Our doubts as arbiters included questions of censorship, pat- or maternalism and ageing vision, for sadly we realize we have become the new old fogies.

While sifting we noticed that the bomb and the dole seldom inspire fresh thoughts, and that neon lighting and over-ripe melons have had their day in the description stakes. We also observed that the punch-line syndrome occurred with alarming frequency: a snappy tailpiece cannot rescue a weakly written item and rarely enhances something good. The quality of writing in *Hard Lines 2* is more than welcome to speak for itself.

Probably the most important lesson writers can learn is how to edit their own work. Although fiddling about has been kept to a permitted minimum, we all got the itch to slash and slice.

> *From east and west the writings flowed,*
> *From south for* Hard Lines 2 *and north.*
> *For those who missed inclusion in this episode:*
> *Start work on* Hard Lines 3 *and so forth.*

Break a few rules.

                                                              IAN X

FOURTEEN

Is love french kisses at bus stops
making old-aged women tuttuttut
through thin dry lipsticked mouths
clutching navy-blue imitation leather
handbags feeling violated
resembling baggy-skinned turkeys.

SUE SAUNDERS

WILLIE

Willie was a bachelor. And proud of it. Sizing up the women as he stalked behind them, looking down his nose at the husband-types.

In the local bar he was king, his own man. He always sat at the best table, waiting alone until the women came, observing each as she entered. Finally a suitable one was found. He pounced, drawing her back, fatally entangled. They never ceased to be attracted by his wit and charm, his little touches of consideration, his politeness and willingness to listen. A real gentleman, he was.

But he could never form a serious liaison. He only ever got as far as warming the pot; he never poured it. The young girls would be completely under his spell. He would take them back to his flat, but nothing ever happened. Too much consideration. A night-cap, the easy talk, the soft music. And then: 'Goodbye! Such a nice evening! See you again some time?'

He was always afraid of them, what they might expect of him, marriage. He backed off, scared, seeking his physical pleasures elsewhere. Ducking down dark alleyways, feet rattling on the cobbles, the red lights flashing on his face.

He went to them at night-time, answering their soft entreaties with a secret smile that did not show his teeth. A real gentleman, he was.

A. R. ATKINS

FOR LORD KITCHENER

When a finger pointed in your
direction
did you ignore it?
Or move aside
and let another Joe Soap
take your portion of lead?
One soul-searching digit
had the desired effect
leading to thousands of one-parent families,
and besides,
it is extremely ill-mannered to point
even at the working classes.
Without that finger I wonder
how many fathers would have seen
their womb-fresh children, if each individual
was left to decide where he would place his windowless
                                                  basement.

LAURENCE CALVERT

SIPPING HEARTACHE THROUGH A STRAW

I'm an alcoholic for your love,
But then I suppose you've heard,
You left me pretty shaken –
Did I ever leave you stirred?
You said we'd drink each other dry,
Seems you're not thirsty any more
And left me amidst the empties
Sipping heartache through a straw.

JULIE MILTON

MARK'S CLOISTER

above Mark's cloister
below San Miniato
olive grove over Arno
viewing the coldness
of Florentine splendour
seeking warmth
cheesecloth-clad scooter girls
skirt mudguard and bumper
flash round
multiple *David* copies
tourist postcards detail cock
under romanesque sun

DAVID BANKS

'Keep running!' cries the red. 'Keep running!' cries the blue. 'Onward over the mountain brim and keep running!' I keep running through the decay that was towns where teeth lie as black on the stump of a firelog as if it were a shop. 'Keep running!' they cry. 'Keep running, for fuck's sake keep running, the yellow is dead and already the snails are eating his noses, keep running, they've got the purple and he's screaming, the green and her children have all been raped and stoned, keep running through where eyes laugh from heaven and churches are barren has-beens of wasteland burnt into the shape of a cross; keep running,' cries the blue. 'Red has fallen and rats gnaw at his faces, hear him screaming?' Blue cries just as the fire lands bare on his belly.

There are only now two of us left, and black has been crying over the death of his loved ones, so he won't get far. My whole body is cracking, my lung is bright crimson, but I must keep running. I watch as they catch black, he struggles in vain, his voice of pity can be heard over the dead schools, the dead trees. 'There's white!' I hear them say, they strangle white very slowly and painfully, then they come after me, they will catch me too and the whole world will grow blind.

TERRY CUTHBERT

THE CARING SOCIETY

The poor old dear who lives up the street
Was mugged last week and knocked off her feet
The youths, they took all her pension
If they're caught, they'll be put in detention
The poor old dear's in a hospital bed
She lies with bandages wrapped round her head
She's been on the news, in every paper
The youths are seen as worse than a raper
She'll have presents and cards, mostly from strangers
The poor old dear didn't know of the dangers

The little old alki of no fixed abode
Was beaten up and left in the road
They won't bother to find the youth
The cops'll say, we've got no proof
The little old alki lies in the cells
Her only comfort's a bottle of Bell's
She won't be seen on the box
Soon she'll have to return to the docks
She won't even be in the local rag
She'll use as a bed, the silly old bag

CAROLINE SMAILES

MARRIED

Two people on their backs stare upward
the lights are off and there's no one else
they puff breath like empty pockets

                that first night
we spoke as if all secrets cracked

he plans a careful poem
she picks her words
treading on eggshell
they do not give

                  in the early days
grinning so hard our smiles ache

they must cut and heal again
like people who stay
turning the ring on his finger
thinking of her

                    ROBERT HAMBERGER

STICKS AND STONES

sticks and stones
might break my bones
but calling names
won't hurt me

call me Cain
I killed my brother
Oedipus
I fucked my mother

call me coward
call me brave
call me master
call me slave

call me saint
or call me sinner
who's the loser?
who's the winner?

am I mad
or am I sane?
give me kindness
give me pain

could be evil
could be sick
does it matter?
what's the trick?

sticks and stones
might break my bones
but calling names
won't cure me

MICK NORTH

BURMA STAR

When I was little, knee-high
to an ice-cream van, I wore
a cowboy suit of blazing
red with yellow buckskin fringes –
a regular Roy Rogers.

My father, smiling,
pinned his Burma Star,
his other bronze medallions,
across my pigeon chest.
Like sheriff's stars I wore them.

I lost the medals, spinning,
falling in a graceful arc,
cut down by phantom gunmen from
a wild, imaginary West.

My father shrugged
and rubbed my hair
and for an instant, in his eyes,
I saw real soldiers coughing
blood-red death within the dark
and steaming jungles
of his past.

PHIL CARRADICE

LITTLE RED RIDING HOOD

He took a child and raped her
Then left her still to die.
Please don't castigate nor condemn him.
Understand him, for he is ill.
The sickness is not with him,
It's ingrained in our 'anything goes',
Do-good, undisciplined world.

One thing is for sure:
You can't ask the dead child for an opinion.
Not to worry, though –
In ten years' time the killer
Will have gained a PhD in philosophy.
Then you'll be able to ask him,
Won't you, you do-gooders all?

Ask him:
What price freedom?
What price discipline?
What price morality?
What price well intended deeds
Of false condonement and understanding?

Dead children?

STEPHEN MADDOCK

THE TYPIST AND THE JUNKIE

In the top floor office of W. Bronson & Son, the typist covers the typewriter and puts away her carbons safely in the drawer.

Down the steps into the cold throbbing street.

Friday night and the city's heart is beginning to pump, purple and vibrant, into the grey streets, lighting up the neon signs and bringing out the take-away hamburger stalls.

The Underground train rocks gently, humming and wheezing through the dark tunnels. The typist sits reading. Shiny brown skins, glossy red lips and pearly-rouged cheekbones cover the pages. Painted faces in painted bars, with painted eyes and painted smiles. Curly locks framing the elfin faces, long sleek hair sweeping behind the pale, elegant ones. Fashion pages where the models are all snake-hips and toothpaste smiles.

> *Come on girl, put away*
> *Your paintbox magazine*
> *It's time that you stopped dreaming*
> *You're here, at Kensal Green.*

In the cold, dark night, her office is now far away and all around is starry, lonely space. It is as if the purple city pulse has dwindled farther and farther away and the thin red veins of the suburbs escape into the dark.

Back to the bed-sitter. Back to the brown-stained ceiling and the Dali poster. The alcove kitchen with the cans of tomato soup and the sliced white bread and the remains of a sweet and sour. Back to the room that is always too small, too crowded and yet always achingly empty.

The man crept into the hall, up the stairs and into your room. He warmed your bed with his body and eased your mind with his head. His body was thin and crippled with junk. His chin dark and unshaven. Hunched spine and pale blue junk-fed eyes that stare at nothing. And yet his sallow hands moving over your back are the best you've ever known.

While you sit typing memos, he waits under the lamp post on the corner of the street, or sips a tequila and orange in the Rose and Crown. Some days he just sits in the Underground station, or buys a magazine and imagines himself tickling the breasts of a huge-nippled beauty with thick, dark pink lips.

The typist is sad today. Jealous of her junkie lover whose days are left open, instead of enclosed in a seven-hour box.

Typewriters, letterheads and pencils,
Syringes, hypodermics and highs,
Telephones, box-files and envelopes,
Dreams of trees and blue skies.

Tea-breaks come and go with their usual powdered milk
*   and tea-bags.*
Banging the keys of the typewriter.
Wishing she was banging him.

Dear Sir, we thank you for your letter of the third inst.
Black letters thunder through her brain.

Down the alley alongside the Rose and Crown, where the smell of stale beer clings to the air and empty bottles line the way. Where the air is sour and the ground stained with the dried yellow remains of last night's vomit and brown glass and green glass and the mongrel without a home for ever chasing a newspaper. Where the taste of waste is bitter in the middle of the night misery.

Here in the gutter died the typist's dreams. Junk dreams.

The Friday night chaos as the revellers tumble from the Rose and Crown. The midnight chase for taxis and coffee stalls and the yellow lights of buses.

Junkie lays in his own excrement and remembers his mother.
That warm pink woman.
In the darkest hour, when the pubs have long since emptied,
Rose and Crown passage groans heavily in its sleep, and
screams with the cats.

On Monday morning the rain fell heavy. The Underground was a solid mass of umbrellas. Silver rain washing heavy over the town.

Rinsing away the debris of the night.
Rinsing away the blood and dirt of the Rose and
    Crown passage.

Rinsing red down the drains.
Rinsing red.
Then pink.
Then nothing.

SHEILA DOLERY

SEE YA

'See ya!'
That's what she said,
And I stared dumbly.
See me?
She never had,
Not what I was really like.
Of course, she had meant
'See you soon.'
All her futile life
She'd been saying
'See ya!' to people,
And they'd invariably thought,
'I hope not!'

CHARLOTTE BROWN

DEATH BED STUDY

Nobody knew where she was really going,
her twisted mouth like half a swastika;
told us nothing of the type of black she was encountering.
She passed orange urine through a catheter, other pipes
and tubes took away more of her independence.
The woman in the next bed was purple;
death is a Mardi Gras of colour;
in a carnival only the fairground horses
show their teeth, asking if the silent crowd
wanted cups of tea, so distorted were the
Sisters of Mercy
in their pantomime dresses.

LAURENCE CALVERT

DON'T COPY

Stop
stabbing yourself out of
self-pity.
Listen to the summer sounds,
laugh at your mistakes,
but live your own life.

Watch my moves
but please
don't copy,
as I feel you are sucking me dry,
and leaving me
with no life.

Take my thoughts for a while
(if you must),
but please return them
unharmed.

By the way,
have you ever been in love?
No?
Well, please don't lie
and say
you have.

LEE BURKE

CHURCHLADIES

Down avenues of manicured limes
Churchladies walk.
Watching the weather, the cracks in the pavement,
Clutching their hymnals
In overworked hands.
Inside the monument
The mice meet the elephants.
The little churchladies are hid behind pillars.
In front of the preacher
The harlequins and hatters
Sing praise to their gods
and think of old sins.
Churchladies ponder
Planning perfection,
Timing their exodus
With nimble precision.
Ten pence to the pardoner,
A smile to a neighbour,
And out of the shelter
Rain or no rain.
Like woodlice they scuttle,
Cast-iron. Identical.
Back to their cast-iron,
Identical cells.
They've been to heaven,
But nobody asks them
Why they came back.
Churchladies
Know.

TIM HATHER

THE FUNERAL OF FATHER

Black.
They all wore black.
Even the cat wore black.

Flowers.
Wreaths of flowers.
Gardens of flowers
for him who only grew vegetables.
Mother.
Mother wept,
forgetting the black eyes he gave her.
And brother,
my brother didn't care
to remember the beatings.
Only I spat on the coffin
as it dropped
and said something
my sister wouldn't tell the vicar,
who, while reading the service,
scratched his nose.
And that was the end of Father.

Back home we drank
the sherry from under the stairs.
Aunt Flo remembered early years
when Father was a lad.
I smiled,
infamous by now
for my lack of gravity.
I smiled and said aloud,
'He was the biggest bastard
you ever knew,'
and then,
as the clock passed one,

they had an honest moment;
nobody denounced
the prodigal son
with his two-tone shoes.
That was the memory of Father.

DENISE KING

THE LANGHAM

The stench of cat piss as I walk up the path.
The sudden shock of seeing an electric bulb.
The colour of Jim Tate's hair, as white as paper promises,
And Moore had dyed his kingfisher blue.
Speccy the Mod sits down by the juke box,
Trying to look cool, 'cos it's what you do.
Then in walks Trudy, pink hair reaching for the ceiling,
Drinking some unknown drink no one has ever heard of,
But she assures us it's quite popular down in London,
And London's cool, and it's what you do.
You fit in if you don't fit in in our Langham,
Looking back to '77, when Punk was Punk.
They play the songs no one else likes to hear,
To try and find their 'lost identity'.
You see Jerry on the door, he is Scottish, so we don't mind if
    he wears make-up.
And Christie plays pool, and tells us all what to do.
He's just finished with Effy, in case she went with someone
    else,
She didn't, but they're finished all the same.
We're all scared of Christie, so Christie's cool,
He's okay 'cos he's cool.
Then in walks the anarchist, he knows what to do,
He tells us it's the system to blame,
He works in the Civil Service, we don't mind,
'Cos anarchy is cool, and it's what you do.
Here comes Hud, this is unusual,
Popped down to London, well, he had nothing to wear,
His girl friend's engagement ring and his girl friend follow,
They have public arguments, and he takes his ring back
    regularly,
He spent forty pounds trying to look cheap, it didn't work.
Booga Benson hobbles in, lost his acid so he says,

And we all sympathize, and he sniffs glue, or soap powder,
    or car tyres, or lamp posts.
He snorts cocaine, attempted suicide twice,
We all envy him,
He is cool, and it's what you do.

LISA CAMPBELL

28TH SEPTEMBER

Your lust
My stupidity
Was all it took
To lose my virginity.

Your longing
My craving
Left me stripped
Of the gift I was saving.

I gave everything
To satisfy your need
Not knowing that
I would be the only one to bleed.

JANE GRIFFITHS

BETWEEN TAKE-OFF AND LANDING

I could die
and the garbled pattern of putrid orange and green
on the back of the seat in front of me
would be my final memory.

The stewardess knows this.
She gazes past us,
smiling at the emergency exit,
miming how to snap on an oxygen mask.
It will drop like some inverted jack-in-the-box
if our startled jet wings slap the ocean.

Masks won't save me.
Neither will this seat cushion,
doubling as a flotation device.
I could die laughing
at that one.

Give me some air instead.
I don't like getting stepped over.
I don't like wondering if there's a tiny camera eye
in this tiny bathroom,
if some bored co-pilot is watching a video-monitor
for terrorists.
I check carefully before unzipping my pants.

The tail end of this ugly metal hull
shudders more emphatically than the front.
Cigarette addicts are segregated here.
They shout to each other through their smoke.

Airplanes are rude.
I could die
and the bickering of that teenage boy
the one who doesn't like his dessert
would be the last thing I'd hear.

There's a four-month-old teacup poodle next to me,
cowering in a Velcroed-shut carrying case.
Its owner's cooing didn't fool me
when the brutal heel of her hand
shoved the bony little creature in there.

I see the poodle floating to earth like a snowflake,
free at last.
The poodle owner,
arms and legs splayed,
and the rest of us,
similarly posed,
are falling more heavily,
cartwheeling through clouds,
as stiff as a giant set of jacks,
thrown into the air by a coughing jet
even before the last meal is served.

LYNN MCGEE

'BUT THE GIRL'S ONLY THIRTEEN'

But the girl's only thirteen,
And the guys all laugh as they pass her around,
Pull her around,
Fooling around,
But the girl's only thirteen,
And her brothers laugh as they pass her around,
Throw her around,
Push her around,
But the girl's only thirteen,
And her father laughs as he knocks her around,
Hits her around,
Keeps her down,
But the girl's only thirteen,
And the businessman laughs as he lays her down,
Lays her,
Pays her,
But the girl's only thirteen as she screams out loud,
No, she's not at school,
She knows the ropes,
She's learned all she needs,
She knows there's no hope.

But the girl's only thirteen,
As she stands in the dock,
Alone in the dock,
Watching the clock,
But the girl's only thirteen and her eyes are so clear,
Back in the home,
Shut in the home,
Locked in the home,
But the girl's only thirteen,
And the wire's knotted tight,

Behind the shut door,
Behind the locked door,
The girl's only thirteen,
As she steps off the chair.

GORDON MELLOR

WRITING ON SKIN

At the asylum
they taught me everything
I liked was dirty
dancing   not wearing a bra

making love   making poems

so I would ball this kid
on the black & white tile
floor of the men's bathroom
staring up underneath a sink

& it was dirty   oh yes   it was dirty

As for my poems
they said why
don't you try leatherwork?
I did & now I love writing

on skin   writing on skin

CLARINDA LOTT

WE'RE BACKING BRITTAN

more prisons! restrain! incarcerate!
protect us from people who don't pay their rates
from vagabonds, vagrants, dogs who foul the pavement
& anyone scrounging on the welfare state
from shoplifters, prostitutes, single parents
people who leave food on the side of the plate
who squeeze the toothpaste in the middle
steal from clothes lines & beg on the street

protect us from anyone who answers back
when stopped on suspicion of being black
save us from drug users, self-abusers
anyone who spits or shows their tits
drunks who shout & throw themselves about
Greenham women, pickets, yobs, louts
& anyone who doesn't like the future we face
a place for everyone & everyone in their place

PAT CONDELL

'SO I SPOKE'

So I spoke –
Forcing the silence, at gunpoint,
From the room.
I lifted out your dusty words
From their hiding-corner of a long dead Thursday
    afternoon,

And laid them out.

We picked them over,
Like poster-children hungry for rice,
And finding none.

Yours an attempt
To wipe clean
The graffitied wall:
Mine an attempt
To underline it all
In bright red aerosol.

Blame had hung on a rusty, festering nail,
And when the time came to take it down,
Neither offered to wear the coat.

So you left –
Me with the words
To smear across my memory,

And the door ajar
For silence to shoot back into the room.

ELAINE KIRKHAM

STREET THEATRE

Voice nearly gone.
That'll please them
who send thugs to frighten off my crowd.
The boy who eats fire draws the people,
then I take over.
I speak their thoughts;
they talk through me. They know that
it's why they run
when the police come.
What do they eat? Like me, tomorrow
with greens and rice.
I use to live on hope. I'm tired.
Even rage won't warm me.
You couldn't feed this life to a dog;
he'd starve. I've taken food from dogs before.
Look at the crowd. They love it
when the boy appears to burn himself.
He's getting uppish,
thinks he's money-maker in the act.
So what he rolls on broken glass, I talk,
spit it out. My turn now. Here's how policemen strut;
you can eat if you've a uniform,
play with your gun in public,
and no one says to put it away,
least of all a priest. Yes, they laugh.
There's a boy I'd like to fuck.
I'll touch his face. I draw their energy,
I feel good now, yes, I am a genius –
this is how a gringo walks, here's a high-heeled lady,
that's it, make them laugh, this one's a lawyer,
here's a judge looking for a bribe,
a politician talking of corruption,
state funds in his pocket taken from starving people.
Why don't they turn us all to soap and lard?

When there's no work, the poor must make a profit
somehow, show they're patriotic,
selling cigarettes, themselves, their sisters,
all good business. Every strike's a hunger strike.
Yes, I have bite, I touch the spot.
I'm a mad dog, I'll bite them all,
army chiefs, the president, the deputies,
the bishops, the owners of the mines
and all their wives, clients of the salons,
hotels casinos, yes, I'll bite them,
bite them all before they shoot me. Thank you, friends.
Thank you for the notes, well, well!
And thank you for the silver, large and small,
and thank you, above all,
for emptying your pockets of all those coppers!

HELENA PAUL

THE FAMILY LEMMING

The conversation bled
upon the carpet.
True, they were smiling,
but so was the
arsenic upon the
empty dinner plates.
True, they were laughing,
but so was the portrait
of the dead uncle.

Comparing battle scars,
last year's share prices,
holidays in India,
vomiting in airport lounges,
they failed to
notice the entrance
of the child prodigy.
Strange, really, as they
were relying on him
to take over from
'Daddy's' heart attack.
Not that he had cared,
he told me,
in between rooms.

In fact, I ended up
owning the family lemming.
I once took him
for a walk off the
edge of a cliff.
He didn't seem
to mind, however.
He wouldn't be returning.

JULIE RUTTERFORD

A BOY'S BEST FRIEND

The exercise book fell open.
Open at a page on which I'd written poems.
Like some comic French detective, you
picked it up, my mother,
scrutinized one poem, then gently closed
the cover.
'What's behind all this, then?'
you asked with arched eyebrows.
'Are you unhappy, then?
You never said, but then you always were
quiet, even as a baby.'
I made some excuse about bad company,
you know, mixing with some of the grammar
school boys, ideas above my station and all that.
You promised not to tell anyone about our little
secret,
but then one Christmas, when you'd had a little
too much to drink,
you dragged me into the family's gaze and said,
'Here, what do you think?
Our Philip's been writing poems, go on, Phil,
read us one.'
Then,
'No need to get upset, dear, it's just a bit
of fun.'

PAUL CAMP

COMPANY KEPT

Company cars – ride
Ride close together
The men that they own
Never stray too far alone

With their syrup-tied throats
And their sweet poison
Their minds hold like a prison
Don't get caught
Registration number fits
Almost anyone.

J.C.

NEON

slut streets
strut
in the sunlight

soul singles
slink into
back flat
basements

*

street beats
radio rhythms
blind silence
on the corner

*

coffee bar
shoulders hunched
marked cards
play
for time

*

bus station empty
the man
clatters teacups
& bawls like a
bomb that broke
in his head

while the dead
beat kids
just wait there
& watch him
& don't even listen
with their eyes
going nowhere
still riding to
cities they never
have been

*

slot machines
eat
nail varnish
& nicotine

no one listens
you're invisible
if you win

*

backcombed hair
slick as
black night
star light
lipstick romance
shivers in the
streetlamp

*

he sticks
his tongue
between
her lips

quick
cigarette sex

juke box
lit
hits suck & roll

*

grey silence
fucks
underneath grey walls
cold concrete floor
gives nothing
back

*

switchblade faces
rip
stiletto silhouettes

down in the dance hall
the jive boys
kiss their razorblades

deserted girls
whisper
in waiting alleyways

*

in the fairground
the black wheel
spins
empty
dawn dust crawls
down the ghost promenade

*

you call this the
blues
the bottle is broken
our bodies are bruised
was this supposed to be
loving
tell us the truth
was it always like this
or did we get used

DAVE WARD

48

THE NORTH WILL RISE AGAIN

The wind blows cold across Ilkley Moor.
The black-pudding factory's closing its door,
shirtsleeves rolled down and cloth caps pulled low,
as the rhubarb plants and the dole queues grow.
It's getting harder to find the price of new clogs.
Peat's unobtainable since they put a nature reserve in the
     local bogs.
You mightn't know it from watching *Coronation Street*,
but the heart of the north keeps missing a beat.

Out beyond the suburbs and the stockbroker belt
north of Watford Gap, where the snows never melt,
where a woman's a woman and a man raises whippets,
where ale's always been real and cricket's still cricket,
the mill might still be satanic and dark
but they've turned it into a multi-storey car park
and the cobbled streets are covered in grass –
it's terribly quaint but watch out for the broken glass.

You can still see washing on lines across the street,
rows of starched collars and the odd nylon sheet,
and housewives in hairnets still natter over fences
in that lovely homely way – no airs or pretences:
'How's your Hilda's insides? Has she had 'em taken out?
I don't think our Albert ever got over his gout.
And I'm so glad Doris is marrying, even though he's a Jew,
she might be only sixteen but it's the decent thing to do.'

The menfolk are down the allotment cultivating onions –
marvellous for the hotpot, not so good for the bunions.
At 12 o'clock it's home again for a dinner of fresh tripe
in mint sauce made of toothpaste, the one with the
    red-and-white stripe.
Afternoons are spent with the pigeons in the loft
(in winter they're up there naked just to show they're not
    soft).
Then it's down the pub for dominoes and a pint,
piss it all out in the ginnel, then home for tea with the wife.

Friday night: it's family night for mother and her brood,
fish and chips for fourteen, the original fast food
served up with bread and dripping and bottles of milk stout
and milk of magnesia for Granma in case she has one of her
    bouts.
After tea we sit round the fire and make our own
    entertainments.
We used to have a telly but we couldn't keep up the
    payments,
so the ferret goes down Dad's trousers and Arthur plays the
    spoons,
we take the comb out of the pawnshop and Grandad gives
    us one of his tunes.
Uncle Bert plays bass with his braces and keeps time with
    his hand –
he's an accomplished musician, plays Beethoven on a
    rubber band.

But times are getting harder in Tetley Bitter land.
The aspidistras are wilting and cannibalism's been banned.
Even the Oxfam shops are on permanent sale,
there's talk of a Tizer drought on an unprecedented scale,
and stocks of Kitekat are running dangerously low –
we'll soon be filling our sarnies with soot-flavoured snow.

50

There's an epidemic of whooping cough spreading west
   from Cleethorpes
and a plague of daddy-longlegs has been spotted heading
   north.

But why am I telling you this? I'm sure you've heard the
   tale.
You've seen *Boys from the Blackstuff*
and your cousin knows Alexei Sayle.
You went for an interview once at Manchester University
and you were terribly shocked at the state of the inner city.
You're researching a new documentary for broadcast on
   Channel 4
about the re-emergence of rickets among Britain's new poor,
and your great-great-great grandfather was born in Heck-
   mondwike,
so you know from first-hand experience what the north's
   really like.

Well, we're extremely grateful for your well-meant concern
and all the opportunities you gave us the chance to earn,
a hundred Oxbridge places a year or our very own Saturday
   night chatshow,
and we weren't to worry about our accents, terribly ethnic,
   you know.
Though we kept the muck while you took the brass,
you were always generous to the working class,
you called us quaint or revolutionary or loyal
and you admired our respect for all things royal.

I hate to have to break this but it's time for us to split.
Thanks for all your help but (to be endearingly blunt) you
   can stuff it.

You've always encouraged us to show some self-reliance:
well, you can keep your southern comfort and your SDP/Lib
   Alliance
and your soft-focus sepia prints of northern moors and dales –
we'll even let you keep the northern half of Wales.
We'll survive on our stockpiles of mushy peas and suet;
we've applied to join the Third World – I hope they'll let us
   do it.
So it's UDI for Yorkshire, self-government for Barnoldswick.
The north will rise again – an autonomous banana republic.

ANDY PEARMAIN

DEBBIE PLAYS ALONE

Debbie plays alone
at Charing Cross.
Beneath the march
of endless feet
from street to tube
and tube to street.

Raped a thousand
times a day,
by every man
who passes by,
touched by every prying eye,
behind guitar
and yellow blouse.

She sits and plays
and sings in time
with Mitchell's verse.
Years between her fingers
and her lips,
creating Nineteen
Sixty-Eight,
   for sixty pence.

PAUL BARRETT

STILL LIFE

this poet is serious, his verbs are
metaphors, his adjectives precise
& unnecessary; he writes in perfect

three-line stanzas like this, he
teaches creative writing, there is
a right way & a wrong way, he teaches

the right way; he brings out a collection
every few years before arriving at
middle age where he has always be-
longed

poetry should not be trivialized
being his reason for breathing, no
never trivialized, it has a noble heart

& function; he has never heard of Bob
Marley; he likes an occasional archaic
turn of phrase, calls it his poetic

licence (you buy it at the post
office & wear it around your neck
in case anyone finds you wandering

in reality); the torn bough, the black
wing – his images are delicate, precise;
when you see him he'll be crouching

at a door marked 'posterity' hoping
someone comes to let him in before
the pubs close & the skinheads arrive

PAT CONDELL

54

'I FELL IN LOVE WITH A BOY FROM JAPAN'

I fell in love with a boy from Japan
And wore sleeves of silk in graceful folds.
Cool evenings were spent, smarting to the taste of salt
                                grasses and *soshi*.
Hours drifted over the sea, a field of blue grasses
Which shed frothed white seeds into the wind
Which rattled through our paper house.

When the hot white flash came and burnt our flesh,
You would see me no more.
Three years later, scarred and bent, I returned home
And you wrote to me in fine black ink on pure white
                                rice paper.

LESLEY WOODS

GO-GO GIRLS

It was a pornographic photograph really,
Though old-fashioned now, and furtive somehow,
Showing a roomful of women undressing,
Old and young alike, all unknowing,
Foreign-looking and sexy.

The camera had obviously concentrated on the young ones,
Especially one with her breasts already uncovered,
But behind her one could see others less attractive,
Some even fat and ugly,
All getting ready for bath night.

There was a lust in the picture and fear as well,
'Cos it was really a forbidden film,
And that randy young guard had truly risked his life to take
    it
When he peered through a 'changing-room' window one
    day
Next door to the gas chambers at Auschwitz.

MASON ABBOTT

'DON'T TURN AND WALK AWAY'

Don't turn and walk away,
Don't turn your back and say nothing,
Don't be so damned assured
Because some day you'll see
that by turning your back it
won't make any difference.

TERESA O'BRIEN

'WITH HER STIFF LITTLE RHEUMATOID FINGERS'

With her stiff little rheumatoid fingers,
Scarred wrists and ex-pink sex-hair,
Viv's sort of SRN and ex-punquette;
The rat race swims through her laddered fishnets.
From Marquee Moon to ward, to bus stop,
From tenement squats and rent-boy flats,
She stares between the slats
Of bamboo blinds and Habitat chairs,
And squints to see Utopia.
      Her back still bruises to the rub of strange floors,
But the deepest, dearest scars are all inside,
Numbed by pints of brown ale and sleeping pills;
Fierce rouged-on weals where I scratch her playfully,
And a graphic designer once tried to enslave her.
      'Oh, I could have died for him,'
She breathes her bruises,
Cries on shoulders on buses,
And chooses which pair of fuck-me shoes
To wear for a drink, a blue funk,
For those dancing, smiling men,
Who appear (and leave her smarting just as quickly);
And with or without her uniform,
With her sharp little Diamon' Deb fingers,
She holds their bodies, cold as cadavers,
And whispers, 'Oh, I could have died for two,'
And nightly does, in the frenzied rub
Of office boys and single beds,
As the benzedrine rush beats time at her breasts,
And of all the dreams she's slept with,
The best is of sweetshops of pills,
A world of liquorice allsort thoughts;
One for each finger that aches less and less,
Immune to the rub of the world and her feelings,
Sighing that where there's a will, please God,

Maybe one day she'll find what she needs,
When I too have left rusting on the heart
That now bleeds on the beds of South London
A graffiti that reads like a bus stop:
    'Oh, I could have died with you.'

NIGEL WOODHEAD

TOO FAST TO LIVE, TOO YOUNG TO WORK

I'm the James Dean of the dole queue
You've got to admire my cheek –
Trying to work out how to live fast and die young
on seventeen-fifty a week.

A legend in my own cubicle
All alone, never one of the mob
I'm the James Dean of the dole queue
A rebel without a job.

MARK JONES

BARTLEBY

Where Bartleby goes
through parks and city streets
no one knows.
Audit clerk Bartleby walks alone,
stares hard at the birds
as the church bells call,
so far away;
soft clang of metal,
click, click, as the typewriter comes to life
beneath his gaze.
Works in his office after dark,
buried amongst filing paper neatly stacked
in his buttoned-up shirt.
And sleeps in his office late at night
after the cleaners have gone –
somewhere outside life passes him by,
struggling beneath suit and expression
something is missing,
but he doesn't know why.
Someone stirs amongst the shadows
beside the coughing that moans the air,
beneath the lamp post
Bartleby goes there;
sees the tramps bound in newspaper upon the pavement,
the rusting ships creeping into harbour by the slums
and early washing line
mingling in with the mist of the foggy city.
Only a roadsweeper upon the kerbside
as the swift street market appears,
but Bartleby sees neither.
So where does the carton in the river go to,
crushed and half-sunk in the cold of the water
until it drowns?

RORY SEAN BINGLEY

AFTER CHRISTMAS

It was very cold.
Beneath the ripped overcoat
his body sagged,
as if he had a broom stale
supporting his back
and hung suspended.

I didn't give him the money,
unusual for me,
not to spare someone the price of a cup of tea,
even when the money's spent on whisky.

It was just after Christmas.
Across the street there was a girl in a shop window
dismantling a Christmas tree.
He looked through me,
as if an armistice
had just ended.

WILLIAM KNOTT

FILE 'S' FOR SCRAP (FILE 'F' FOR FREE)

A woman called today,
Quiet and concerned,
From the DHSS.
A battered black briefcase,
Containing many lives,
Including mine.
She smiled and asked to sit
And sitting
She opened her satchel
And took out my life
in all its leafy coloured splendour.

'Just a few questions,'
As all that was me
Passed between us,
In yes and no,
In countless little boxes,
A cross, a tick,
A scribbled note,
As I was assembled,
Bit by bit,
Before our weary gaze,
For other distant eyes
To nod and know
And fit me in my place
Between the ticked-box lives
Of my faceless, fearless race.

'We like to know.'
She smiled and turned a page,
The pen skipping,
Dipping,
Riding on,
As my ego boldly tripped

On the dots along the lines,
To leave me hanging in the spaces
Between my silent words.

Am I done?
I thought,
Signing in the gap marked 'X'.
Is this my glowing testimonial,
My mark upon the earth?
There should be more
To a life not yet begun,
Above the path
That leads me on,
That beckons me to follow,
A path so narrow
And inevitable,
So precise and uninspired.

SIMON LINDLEY

SQUARE PEG

Nobody told him it was Saturday
Rooted to his spot on platform three
All wound up and ready to be
In motion at the turn of a key.

Nobody told him it was Saturday
A grey thumb stuck out on the station
Somehow, something fouled up the routine
Right suit, wrong day, right location.

Nobody told him it was Saturday
Season ticket held firmly in his pocket
Clean white shirt and shiny shoes
Stood waiting for the eight o'clock rocket.

Nobody told him it was Saturday
Briefcase and patience wearing thin
A square peg stuck in a round hole
A sardine exiled from the tin.

Nobody told him it was Saturday
Batteries not yet up to full charge
Realization sinking, slowly, in
A red face not enough camouflage.

Nobody told him it was Saturday.

MIKE GODDARD

'IN A BLACK SLEEPLESS LIMBO'

In a black sleepless limbo
      wolf-worries circle the fire of my thoughts.
Feeling like a boarding-house of sad tenants –
      the clocks have stopped,
         the telephone is broken
            and there's nothing to do
               but look in the mirror.
Hostile faces sneer on my mental screen
      and troubles that shun daylight
         rise to trumpet their nocturnal victory.
The conscience accountant sends his final demand.
A friend's idle comment becomes the centre of the world –
      under brilliant scrutiny the words expand spongily
         beyond comprehension.
The teddy bear of Jesus holds out his hands
      but the monster of night crawls onward
         till a tinkling milkfloat signals dawn's reprieve.

IAN MOLE

LOVE POEM

Leaving the room while you undressed
was a bad start
but you looked OK when I came back in,
with the sheets pulled up to your chin.

And it was all going to be such good fun,
and you smelt so nice
then I cracked a nervous joke
about body lice
and ran out of things to say.

Five years later, sharing a warmer bed,
having discovered something
of what happens
after everything's been said,
I pull the sheets up to my chin
and wait for my lover to come back in.

MARTIN EDWARDS

I DON'T WANT DIANA IN THE PALACE

with her needles and blood,
soaking in the tub 3 hours
rubbing vitamin E into
her skin   you can fuck any
one   bring anybody here
but I don't want to have to
take care of both of you

Blonde hair and nothing
else under it, I'm warning
you   I'll write the porn
books I love you and hate
it that you're dying   anyone but
that woman with her snow
and tracks   she's like a piece
of furniture that leaves
a stain   bring someone else

into bed so we can make it
anyone but her   I'll leave
I never wanted 50 rooms of
carved ebony the jewelled
glass is damp from the sea
leave Diana in her tower
These rooms stink of the dog
I can't type with the two
of you moaning doves in
the olives won't muffle it
the white sheet with your
blood on it isn't bright enough

LYN LIFSHIN

LUCIFER IS LAUGHING AT US

'And Jesus told us to trust in the Lord our God,'
Said the black-hatted evangelist in Leicester Square
But all we did was stare.
Then we went underground
But where the train should have been
We found
'Someone has gone under a train'
Chalked on a blackboard, like one equals none.

'Assaults on staff . . .' began the poster on the wall –
Have you ever watched it happen?
'If you see a suspicious package . . .'
Go on PICK IT UP
It might
Be a little less pain
Than going under the train.

ANNE DIXEY

THE ACTRESS

Now the stage is bare.
Tonight I sang my songs for you,
You laughed and clapped as audiences do
And I knew you cared.
And then you all stood up for me,
And I stood and cried for all to see
And now the stage is bare.

You've all gone home now
Left me standing alone,
Tears still in my eyes
Memories of ovations and pale pink carnations
And worthless goodbyes.
And then it all comes back to me,
Flushed faces in my mind I see,
So real I stretch out to touch you there,
But I'm still alone,
And the stage is bare.

LISA CAMPBELL

FIRST MOVE

on sticky summery days i
liked to sit at that sunset sidewalk café watching
boys strut back and forth their
tight jeans bringing this angel
to her knees
     one caught my eye as his certain
     footsteps brought him nearer my
     god to me
         hearing his earrings clatter i watched
         his swagger seesaw his pockets down
         the street motionless
         at my spot my whole body sighed begging
         for just one chance

PLANET CLARE

THE SAFE SOLUTION

He wakes to the sound of rain on the window, lies still behind the drawn curtains listening to his own heartbeat, the alarm brings in the morning with a clatter. Eventually he will clock in, after the toothpaste, razor, soap and breakfast ritual. He'll clock in at three minutes to six exactly, pour a steaming cup of hot liquid that incites memories of real tea, lighting the first cigarette, that trembles in his fingers. Bleary-eyed good-morning voices clutter the air, morning-lagged workmates crumple into chairs like filter-tips into ashtrays, stunned but revived by distant machinery as it groans and churns in anticipation.

One shift on,

One shift off.

Then into the changing room and wall-to-wall smiles of naked page-three girls, eager to arouse, but it's too early and besides he's come here to work. Shortly he will secure his throne at the head of his one-man-operated wonderland of nuts and bolts jokingly called a machine, a showcase of man's bizarre talent for devising uncannily ugly machinery for desperately boring jobs. The excitement won't kill him but it'll keep the wife off his back and feed the dog. Besides eight hours is only a third of a day (a third of a lifetime). And passes . . . quickly enough.

So he clocks off, makes his way home through the pleasant concreteness of the town, takes in the graffiti-lined subways, feeling dirtier than the drains, passes through the shopping centre with its afternoon stampede of mothers, prams, truants and young unemployed. He wonders why kids today dress so funny and never seem to smile, then he realizes that he isn't smiling either.

He arrives home, kisses the wife though he sleeps alone, pats the dog, pushes off his boots and airs his socks. Small talk ensues with the immortal lines, 'Had a nice day?' slotted between potted history, supermarket scandals. He answers with a safe but dishonest 'Yes' and nods his head in all the right places.

Teatime passes cushioned from conversation by the television, with its dismal soap-opera ethic of a cleaner-than-clean world where every problem has an answer or at least a five-year guarantee, by the newspaper and its neatly Thalidomized dialogue warped snugly to the shallow contours of the public mind, by his own inadequacies, a pressure cooker looking for a safety valve.

He thinks he's found it as he escapes, clean as a newscaster, to the brimming club, a last male refuge, the soothing brew, tasting of wood, a gradual blurring of the senses that slurs his voice but not enough to turn his stale breath from the barmaid whom he pulls as regularly as she pulls pints.

Then there's the wife at home, disappointed in her semi-detached, expensively decorated cell. He'll return to her when the club or its barmaid turfs him out. And he'll cry for sex and fall asleep on top of her, and she'll put up with it because she's got nowhere to go and besides he says he loves her.

Both avoiding a change, trying to find happiness with false loyalties and a safe solution.

KEVIN CADWALLENDER

SUBURBIA ROAD

Where barrel-chested houses sleep tucked up
In established green,
Roofs glint after rain like
Otters' backs.

Lawns are freshly laundered & each leaf of
Privet is creased & clean.
Puddles flash fragments of images in the road. They
Are scattered like a torn photograph.

Sticking from the mouths of unopened doors
Are newspaper tongues.
Inside the bleary readers keep their open secrets
Like toenails under the pillow.

Here milk bottles with notes in are only
Jokes of bombs –
Concern is for the youngest who studies rabbits
In the butcher's window.

By & large you are safe (as the houses)
Where you pose no threat;
Getting on with (the neighbours)
Fortune & overtime.

Soon a work day will start & the gate will
Shed the dawn's cool sweat.
The drive will dry & the white stone chips will
Not model the stars' dot-to-dot signs.

Yesterday I saw a totter's horse & cart parked
Like a car in the road.
The scrap was piled delicately high
Like a sculpture.

The beast buffed its harnessed neck against a lamppost.
Shook. Settled. Its itch controlled . . .

STEPHEN CLARKE

AND THEN YOU CALLED

When I opened the curtains this morning
Someone had painted every cloud black.
There was a notice on my window:
BASTARD! it read in your lipstick.
I wondered why you left by the window
And asked for Sellotape instead of a kiss.
The sparrows were in raincoats.
There was a gang of bus inspectors on the corner,
Practising creeping up on people from behind.
I went downstairs to put the radio on.
You had suffocated it with a plastic bag.
Seven mirrors lay broken on the floor.
On the note attached you hoped from the heart
That that would be enough bad luck
To be going on with for the time being –
And, no, you didn't want to do it with ice cream.
I heard a knock at the front door.
I welcomed you in for a minute.
You offered me a smile and a letter:
'How about strawberry flavour? Love, Julie.'
I went to work feeling as horny as a cornet.

DAVID CLARKSON

COPIOUS NOTES ON HOW TO CONDUCT ONE'S BEHAVIOUR BY A PRECOCIOUS NOBODY

mustn't hold hands; mustn't make a noise; mustn't play up;
mustn't make a noise; mustn't play up; mustn't sleep in the
   day;
mustn't make people laugh; mustn't make a noise;
mustn't play up; mustn't roll your eyes; mustn't be naughty;
mustn't play with your penis; mustn't make a noise;
mustn't stay still; mustn't eat too fast; mustn't make a noise;
mustn't fart too loud; mustn't make faces; mustn't make
   strange
noises; mustn't make people cry; mustn't play up; mustn't
play with fire; mustn't look at girls; mustn't make a noise;
mustn't roll your eyes; mustn't be a nuisance; mustn't
make a mess on the floor; mustn't make a noise.

> *Protest and survive*
> *reason against tyrannies*
> *bikers against magistrates*
> *the challenge of new poetry*
> *E. P. Thompson at Glastonbury*
> *the challenge of being open*
> *the learning process*
> *the light of light beyond light*
> *which refuses to be read.*

mustn't talk about South African politics, the neutron bomb;
mustn't mention thinking things through, how things
connect, how things work, how true the 7.84 Theatre
Company, Jacques Lacan's discovery of the Mirror Phase,
Steve Varney's running are; mustn't consider the possibili-
ties of an improved anarchist critique of Marxist politics;
mustn't consider spiritual problems, emotional problems,
problems, problems; mustn't even consider for a moment
the possible effects of re-thinking the concept of politics and

the confrontation of apathy; mustn't mention the protective and cowardly people that guard, beat, maim the inmates of special hospitals – these abnormal offenders, the petty criminals, arsonists, alcoholics, sex and violence cases, the casualties of the sixties expansion; mustn't ask to research or film in these sadistic towers; mustn't mention that they are haunted by nurses with neuroses, behaviourists with blindnesses and doctors without minds; mustn't mention successive governments' refusal to cure mental illness; mustn't mention the chemical-technological erosion of the countryside; the realist myth of the television set, the complete dissolution of royalty who attack the unemployed rather than the economic policy; mustn't mention the rags and riches story of Britain in 1981.

DAVID CADDY

POOR LITTLE RICH GIRL

Tasted oil wells, Swiss schools, frogs' legs,
Cartier, carnivals, names.
Countries become dead.
No longer the apple of daddy's eye,
but some rich man's piece of meat.
Searching, searching with plastic bicycle rides.
I WANT – so you have.
Challenge, newness, where? – Cold statues.
Stroke of the hair, eyes that meet an instant too long,
soft tears.
Try a timetable.
A sales assistant, a room in Kiev.
Newness dies, hearts sink, hands held out.
A quiet cottage misted tightly round with greenness.
Friends with flowers . . . but where is your gold mine?
People read, stare, admire, pretend.
Paper notes quick – grab – tear.
'I know her' . . .
Paris Match, the *Tatler*.
Smiles, yachts, suffocate you.
Beneath the make-up hands stretched out – a solitary tear.
Six layers of thick, tight flesh, alienated from the rest.
Deutschmarks change.
Silver round coins with heads – dead.
A battle of kings and tramps.
No huge ships
just a rose petal with thick blue seas.
A gust of wind.
A stroke of thunder . . .
A friend?
Um . . . I understand.

LUCETTE KOVATZIS

DEBS

and I remember
  my first burn

thought I looked magic I did
  with a face like Bugs Bunny in a carrot patch

and I remember
  and I remember
the electricity in my chequered-cool longers
  pretending I had a headache
sittin' in the corner of the room
  one nervous ninny
the Anadins sticking to the roof of my mouth
  having never swallowed them
chokin' like a great thick twit
  rather than dance
in the fast set

and I remember it
  giggling
my first slow dance
  in Brian McLoughlin's house
Cat Stevens' 'Moonshadow'

she was small
  and when she looked up
my shoes turned into sneakers
  as we kissed
my blood yahooin' all over the place
  and my heart
boom boom boom bish bang wallop
  can't you hear them
ding dong ding dong
  the big bells

shaking
  shaking
I remember shaking
  in her arms
holding on
  holding on
we were both
  holding on for dear life
holding on
  holding on
'I've been dreamin' of a Moonshadow
  leapin' and hoppin' on a Moonshadow . . .'

I remember
  I remember it
dribbly dribbly
  the first time
I ever kissed
  I remember

and then

running my hand through hedges
  all the way home

MARK BARRY

'THERE AMONG THE OLIVES'

There among the olives are the idle workmen.
The master's gone, they've gathered in a knot
dappled with sunlight through the grey-green leaves,
quiet and still. What thought has struck them?
What grave conjecture holds them captivated?
These are rebels who've lived in palaces,
torn up the floors of ballrooms when their women slipped
barefoot on the polished wood. They've led their horses
up wide colonial staircases and stabled them
in damask bedrooms, leading them to drink
from marble bathtubs which they scorned themselves.
They've bivouacked in salons, lit their fires,
though never in the fireplace, and, eyes red with smoke,
they've wasted bullets shooting chandeliers,
letting out the music in them as they shattered.
They've warmed themselves at burning libraries
and cooked tortillas by the heat
of smouldering astronomy, mathematics and religion,
flaming geology, fantastic bestiaries and music books,
and all the standard classics bound in leather,
all this impartially, cursing no more than the lack of salt.
Now they seem humble, still, still silent.
One has his head buried in another's shoulder,
two are back to back. One turns a little,
as if abstracted. They hang together, yet seem
utterly detached. They don't betray
awareness of proximity, as if their thoughts
had made them forget everything, heads on one side,
faces dark with effort. In the alien city,
the first time they saw a fire engine,
they shot the monster. In shop windows
they set eyes on what they'd never dreamed of.
This olive grove is more like home,
but is such silence natural to them? Not quite silence.

There's a sound of flies and many at their mouths,
yet all their arms hang limp. Who will cut them down?
Where are their mourners or their murderers?
They picked up guns and died, not worth a bullet.

HELENA PAUL

'YOU GAVE THEM CARE'

You gave them care
   when they were growing,
But it wasn't love
   that you were showing,
The kids need your help
   that's what you said,
But were you willing
   to let them into your bed?

SHAUN ENGLAND

CONTRIBUTORY NEGLIGENCE . . .

In an infamous and extensively reported court case a High
Court judge ruled that a woman who was hitch hiking late
at night and was picked up and raped was 'asking for it'
and guilty of contributory negligence. Angered beyond
belief I wrote this allegorical rant about a high court judge
who picks up a hitch hiker late at night and gets beaten
up . . .

Hitching up the M11
coming back from an Upstarts gig
got picked up 'bout half-eleven
by this bloke in a funny wig
flash Mercedes, new and gleaming
deep pile seats and deep seat piles
I got in and sat there scheming
while the fat cat flashed me smiles

Told me he was back from sessions
with a load of Whitelaw's hacks
told me he'd made no concessions
to the bootboys and the blacks
said he thought that it was stupid
fuss 'bout rapists on the news
bloke was only playing Cupid
girls like that they don't refuse

Asked me if I thought him enemy
asked me if I bore a grudge
told me that he came from Henley
said he was a High Court judge
I asked him to stop a second
'Need a slash,' that's what I said
when he did the anger beckoned
and I smacked him in the head

took the keys and took his money
smashed the car into a ditch
though he moaned, 'They'll get you, sonny!'
got away without a hitch
I don't think they'll ever find me
'cos I'm many miles away
but if one day they're right behind me
I know what I'm gonna say –

He asked for it! He's rich and snobbish
right-wing, racist, sexist too!
Fat and ugly, sick and slobbish
should be locked in London Zoo!
He wanted me to beat him up!
It was an open invitation!
Late at night he picked me up –
an act of open provocation!

High Court judges are a blight
they should stay at home in nice warm beds
and if they must drive late at night
should never pick up Harlow Reds!
A fivepence fine is right and proper
and to sum up my defence
it was his fault he came a cropper
contributory negligence!

ATTILA THE STOCKBROKER

ROMANCE

I met him at a party,
You know the sort I mean,
Where everyone gets drunk
Because they're young.
In all innocence
I walked with him
Along the railway sidings,
And was soon expecting his baby.
He said he'd marry me
When I told him,
That was in the queue
At the fish-and-chip shop.
He'd just been in a fight
And his lip was bleeding.
He said he loved me
And I said I loved him.
And now I'm married
With a baby daughter
And we live with my mother
Because my husband's left me
And gone off with another.

JANE GRIFFITHS

MEMORIES

When I heard your voice
Above the crowd it made me crawl,
Like a ghost from its shroud.

Could this be the start of it again?
Could this be the chance to get by
Without the pain?

I took the chance and called you over.
Above the crowd you stood head and shoulders.
Your hair looks fine but you look older.

We got to talking over old times,
Of past love and bedroom crimes.
It was then I realized why we had to part:
Your body's beautiful but you've got no heart.

ROBERT DAINES

SKIN VEHICLE

09.39
See the screen
see the two dogs fucking
locked up tight and shamed together
unique in private pleasure
like billions before them
they hop on through the courtiers' waltz
they play the secret farce

men women oxen pigs and wildebeest
all so sure that they alone
are the sole sweat discoverers
in this carnal world

promises made and trashed
inches pushed and sucked on
lay them end on end and see how far they stretch
these elastics of illusion

10.07
Warm and wet
in slippiness I grow
bent over
bunched
a shoemaker without fingers

I am passive kicking
as actions course on through this tissue

the natal sickness
waking up to nausea and the porcelain thrill
mid-morning cooking sherries that float on through the
    membrane
in cheap alcoholic osmosis
the stomach-ache powders that she swallows so fast

and the stairwell brinks of her Valium daze
I feel the long hot baths
have bad sleep dreams of steel sharp needles knitting
sense his drunken fingers search inside
hear the slurred late evening promises
'One gut punch can end it all'

worry wrinkles crease from the first formed heartbeat

10.20
I get bigger and mean
kicking and cursing
making her stoop with my weight
she carries on expectant
with this child up front
with a shopping bag on either arm

climbing the stairs
pushing through the door
she slumps to an armchair with her overcoat on

it is birthday
time to go
vacate depart

she lights a cigarette
coughs out smoke and spit

she goes to the bedroom
takes a pill bottle from the cabinet
swallows down some capsules and sinks on to the bed

she hears the telephone calling
but doesn't move

it stops

as she cradles her stomach
frozen meat in her shopping bag begins to defrost
in the kitchen milk is going sour
her fists clench as the phone begins again

she knows it will be soon

11.18
Stony seeds
some risen some shocked
unfold this spittled fate
out of the shell and into the breeze
through the stitched sad wound and into sharpest tiled light
I am swaddled and layered like a cutting under glass
she is monitored and washed
we are equally bewildered

soon sent back to climb the stairs
to soak up noise and wet this baby's head

I wail
and the damp reflexive language
runs like melted glaze
down this boiled Dresden face

I am potted and days old
septic and ripe

12.45
This room smells of paintbox colours
building bricks and the bottled breaktimes milk
I am in the aisle
stumbling through words
in some halting description of peasants and witches
of trials by fire

laughter beats with my broken syllables
but a lady teacher with lank thin hair
leaves me to struggle alone though the minutes

in bright-eyed shame
with a face spiked red
I give out and grind to my halt

she stands behind me
gathering tension with her breath on my neck
we wait

out of the stillness comes the thinnest of streams
the class stare as pale urine soaks the flesh of my leg
falling and dripping to the wool of my knee-sock

I am motionless
rooted
as a stain grows like blood on the groin of my shorts
as a white child's leg marbles yellow

already a shallow puddle has formed at the sole of my shoe
in a slow strong voice I hear her call:

'Wipe it up
use your hands'

on the waxed scuffed floor
I handprint piss
I learn the lesson of a builded brick

14.00
Television box all day all night
I can dream wires better than mothers
seven-foot colour screens bank against the walls
solar-powered generators send out roof-panelled pictures

we are remote-controlled in three four five dimensions
we have vision speakers with cables like chains
like a steel grass world
pre-programmed cameras sensitive to light and heat
feed my magnesium tubes
volume controls are always high
colours stay distorted
tape computers radios and record decks
amplifiers and interference dishes
my mixed-mesh floor is littered with pyrotechnic junk
water-cooled clocks and concrete fridges
fusion face-lifters all set to automatic
micro-waves stand stacked in every corner
there are life supports beneath my rubber bed
wrapped inside the casing of a dialysis machine . . .

I have a child's view
I have the blankest dream

I am the miracle of spare-part surgery
with a double-speed memory and built-in picture search
ears a thousand watts per channel
both blue eyes ranged telescopic
sixty-one bones in each foot
pre-cast in high-tensile steel

all the fingers on my left hand are nuclear . . .

with a churned packed brain
pressed in offal
little more than low-grade dogfood
I am the proto-type success
a model from your production line
that rolls mechanically on
spewing legion numbers for the class on zero-zero
the fuck-up fraternity
soon to be committing cinema in a suicide near you . . .

14.31
Manoeuvring from cushion to couch
lights go out in one quick sweep
there is a falling down
a fumble and advance

ignore the wails and warnings
here comes floodtime
as a virgin's last inhibition overflows
and a small boy's river starts to break
against clenched sad muscles

with clothes off
and make-up disappeared
her limp child's body comes clammy and cold

no matter
no time

14.47
Older on the tide
bleeding and forlorn
she shakes to the rhythm of afterbirth

lying belly on belly with the fractured girl
I am careless and dismissive
wanting something rented that will smile on cue
with hard stone rivets for her puppy eyes
with a slab where her mouth should be

by morning I am glad and gleaming
eager for the factory
to shout and find another
to get some practice in

15.16
Yes I've seen them
pram pushing through the council streets
to ten-foot queue at the early morning butcher's
their slow young husbands are out of work
at home in bed asleep

these women are the already quiet
in their cheap slack printed dresses
never thinking of biology days
and their embarrassed third-form laughter

I am the clever boy
with a pin face looming
cruel and blind
blind and blind

15.50
Working and waiting and wanting

my father wanted riches but was scared of the money
wanted sweet young girls but dreaded their mothers
wanted dark pilot's glasses but ended short-sighted
for years his hopes piled up high
like uncollected rubbish
and sometimes when the wind is right
you can smell them rotting there unspoken:

'Forty good years in the paint factory
overtime and holidays
forty good years in the paint factory
like father like son my son'

DAVID WALSH